WATER VOICES

G. P. PUTNAM'S SONS • NEW YORK

TOBY SPEED ILLUSTRATED BY JULIE DOWNING

When you wake to the banjo strumming of frogs
and the lake is a silky soup
where turtles dive from island-logs
and herons glide and dragonflies skate
and faraway ripples from distant oars
make their slow voyage out,
I trail my white net over the lake
and wait for sunrise.

Who am I?

I am Morningmist-
doing a disappearing trick.

When the slide's so hot it burns your legs
and dogs pant
and Popsicles drip,
when carrots nap in the garden
and kittens in the shade
and fans do a slow dance on tabletops,
I whirl like a string of pearls in the yard.

Who am I?

I am Sprinklerspray.
Want to play?

When you wear barefoot shoes with seaweed laces,
sand mittens and saltwater socks,
when shells gleam and striped umbrellas squat
and sea gulls wade in my foam,
I chase you and I roll away!
Catch your ankles and roll away!
And then I eat your sand castle for lunch.

Who am I?

I am Oceanwave.
Watch out, I'm hungry!

When lights flicker
and afternoon pretends to be night,
when trees groan and leaves bristle and snap
and the wind moans low in warning,
when the radio crackles
and crickets quit
and every blade of grass stands still,
I rush in stamping and throwing darts.

Who am I?

I am Thunderstorm.
I start with a rumble and end with a rainbow.

When worms wriggle up from the earthy deep
and trees drink
and petals shine,
when twigs float in rivers around your boots
and you feel the spray of cars galoshing by,
I ripple and wrinkle to show the sky
how it looks upside down!

Who am I?

I am Mudpuddle.
Jump over me.

When pillows look for pillowcases
and in the evening cars roll by
with grown-up people going places,
when your fingers wrinkle
and the soap slips
and waves make little plishings
and all the hard parts of the day
go sailing off in cups and scoops,
I hold you close in my lap.

Who am I?

I am your Bedtime Bath.
Have a splash.

When your smile is dozy drowsy
and your eyelids buttered with sleep,
when the moon curls up like a cat in your quilt
and all the shooing wind shivers away
and the streetlamps wear halos
and moths tap their secret codes on screens
and stars wink
and the curtains spread their wings and try to fly,
I drift down from the sky and lick the grass.

Who am I?

I am Dew.
In the morning I'll be gone.

In memory of my father—T. S.

For Mary East,
who inspired me to draw—J. D.

Text copyright © 1998 by Toby Speed
Illustrations copyright © 1998 by Julie Downing
All rights reserved. This book, or parts thereof,
may not be reproduced in any form without permission
in writing from the publisher.
G. P. Putnam's Sons, a division of The Putnam & Grosset Group,
200 Madison Avenue, New York, NY 10016.
G. P. Putnam's Sons, Reg. U.S. Pat. & Tm. Off.
Published simultaneously in Canada. Printed in Singapore.
Designed by Donna Mark. Text set in Bryn Mawr Book.
Library of Congress Cataloging-in-Publication Data
Speed, Toby.   Watervoices/Toby Speed;
illustrated by Julie Downing. p. cm.
Summary: Illustrations and descriptive text present water
in some of its many forms: morning mist, sprinkler spray,
a thunderstorm, and a bedtime bath.
[1. Water—Fiction.]   I. Downing, Julie, ill.   II. Title.
PZ7.S746115Wat 1998 [E]—dc20 95-10588 CIP AC
ISBN 0-399-22631-1

10 9 8 7 6 5 4 3 2 1

First Impression